crest

This ~~book~~ belongs to...

_____

_____

_____

_____

The Very Best Beast
An original concept by author Alison Green
© Alison Green, 2022
Illustrated by Siân Roberts
Represented by Plum Pudding Illustration Agency
Illustrations © Siân Roberts, 2022

MAVERICK ARTS PUBLISHING LTD
Studio 11, City Business Centre, 6 Brighton Road,
Horsham, West Sussex, RH13 5BB, +44 (0)1403 256941
© Maverick Arts Publishing Limited 2022
Published June 2022

A CIP catalogue record for this book
is available at the British Library.

ISBN 978-1-84886-806-9

For Dan, the very best brother – S.R.

For Mum and Dad – A.G.

Maverick
publishing

www.maverickbooks.co.uk

The Very Best Beast

written by Alison Green
illustrated by Siân Roberts

There once was a kingdom that spread far and wide,

Where the newly crowned king ruled with courage and pride.

And the new king announced, "I shall hold a contest –

To find the best beast for my **new royal crest**!"

So he summoned all beasts to his great castle hall,
To find out **the very best beast** of them all.

"Pick me!" said the owl. "I'm most terribly **wise**,

Ask me some questions. I'll soon win the prize."

"What about me?" boldly called out the swan,

"Look how my neck is so **graceful** and **long**."

"You're not all that special," a young rabbit jeered,

"What use is your neck if you don't have **long ears**?"

"Your Highness!" the fox sighed, "I'm cunning and quick.
I'm shrewd and I'm brave, Sir, it's me you should pick."

The lion roared, "Nonsense! It's easy to see,
There's no other animal **braver** than me."

"Choose me!" growled the tiger,
"Just look at my **claws**."

But the crocodile snapped,
"Mine are **longer** than yours."

Now, because of her size, you'd be right to assume,

That they all saw the elephant inside the room.

But the elephant felt **far too shy** to compete,

So she stood at the back, looking down at her feet.

She feared that the others would laugh at her size,

Or her big **flappy** ears, or her **wobbly** thighs.

So she quietly watched as one beast, then the next,

Tried hard to convince the king they were **the best**.

Then, just as the crocodile finished his bragging,

The doors were thrown open and in flew a **DRAGON**!

"I'm here," roared the dragon, "to claim the royal prize!

There's no other beast with my **power** or **size**."

"That's true," said the king. "You have much to admire."

Then the dragon's mouth opened, and out came...

...REAL FIRE!

"**HELP!**" cried the swan, "I'm too **gorgeous** to die!

Though I'm sure I would make the most perfect swan pie."

The rabbit shrieked, "Don't let that fire near my ears!"

Whilst the lion and tiger both **burst** into tears.

Then the terrified animals ran for the door,

Knocking the king and his throne to the floor.

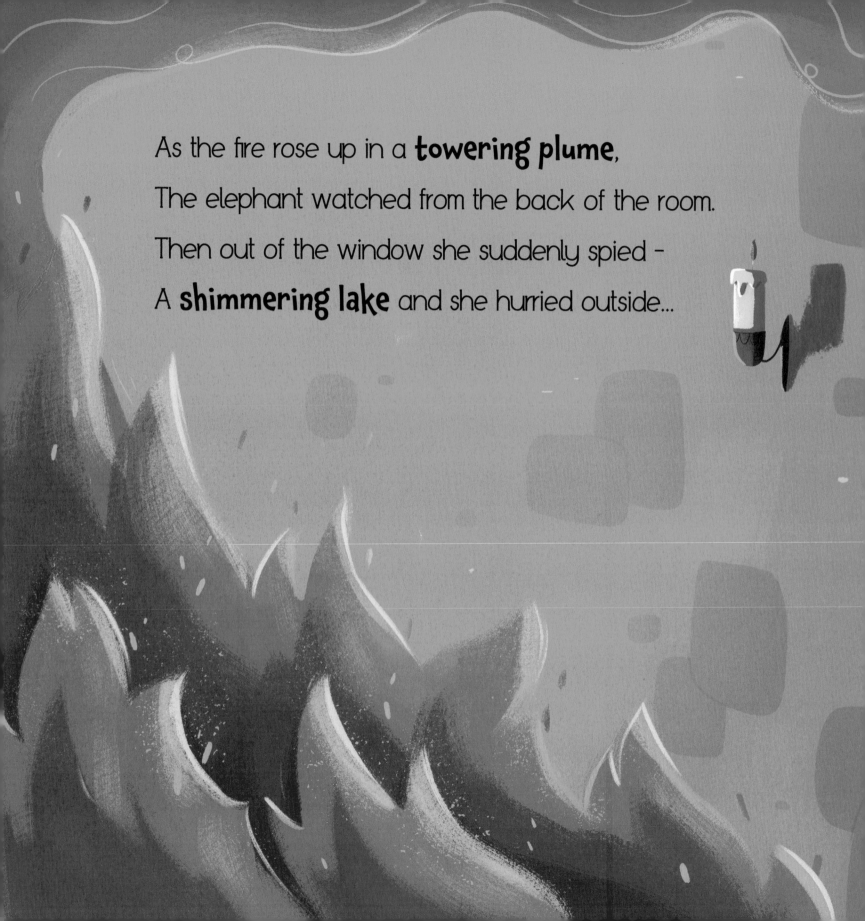

As the fire rose up in a **towering plume**,

The elephant watched from the back of the room.

Then out of the window she suddenly spied –

A **shimmering lake** and she hurried outside...

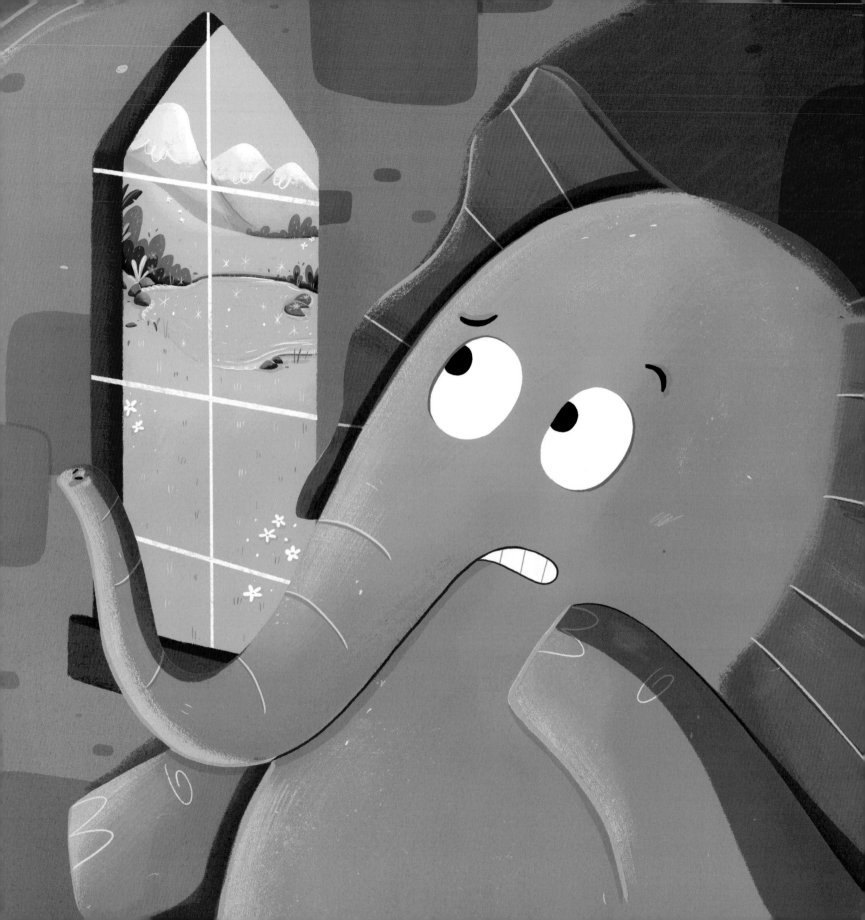

She drank up as much as her trunk could contain,
And **squirted** the water out over the flames.

They **spat** and they **sizzled** and finally went out.

"Our lives have been saved!" came a jubilant shout.

"**BRAVO!**" cried the king as he got to his feet.

"My castle is saved and my contest complete.

This wonderful elephant **wins by a mile!**

She's **clever** and **brave** and I do like her **style**."

Then the king held a party most **splendid** and **grand**,
And everyone came from all over the land,

To cheer for the beast that had truly impressed,
And to watch the reveal of the **new royal crest**.

"This marvellous beast saved us all!" the king gushed,

And everyone bowed as the elephant blushed.

"You're **fearless** and **smart** and I must say, **quite cool**,

I'd love you to stay here and help me to **rule!**"

At the royal request, the elephant stayed,

And remained with the king as his new royal aide.

And the king and the elephant **ruled side by side,**
From the throne of the kingdom that spread far and wide.

The End